E
Sta   Star Wars: the mystery of
           the rebellious robot

DATE DUE			
JY 13 '89	AP 07 '99		
JY 28 '89	MR 28 '00		
AG 21 '90	JE 25 '02		
SE 6 '90	JY 02 '02		
AL 31 '95	JY 09 '02		
NOV 30 '95	JE 02 '04		
JUL 03 '95	AG 18 '05		
AL 19 '98	EE 0 4 '09		
AL 06 '98	OC 2 4 '15		
JUL 16 '98	NV 15 '16		
AUG 20 '98	OC 01 '16		
OCT 08 '98	JE 05 '01		

201-9500   PRINTED IN U.S.A.

MEDIALOG
Alexandria, Ky 41001

STAR WARS™

THE MYSTERY OF THE REBELLIOUS ROBOT

STAR WARS™

THE MYSTERY OF THE REBELLIOUS ROBOT

illustrated by Mark Corcoran

Random House 🏠 New York

Copyright © 1979 by Black Falcon, Ltd. All rights reserved under International and Pan-American Copyright Conventions. Published in the United States by Random House, Inc., New York, and simultaneously in Canada by Random House of Canada Limited, Toronto. *Library of Congress Cataloging in Publication Data:* The Mystery of the rebellious robot. (Star Wars) Summary: Luke Skywalker and his companions are puzzled by the sudden bizarre behavior of their robots and the malfunction of their machines. [1. Science fiction] I. Corcoran, Mark. II. Series. PZ7.M9973 [Fic] 78-19703 ISBN: 0-394-84086-0 (trade); 0-394-94086-5 (lib. bdg.). Manufactured in the United States of America.   3 4 5 6 7 8 9 0

77991

In a distant galaxy, in another time, a pilot named Han Solo pointed his starship, the *Millennium Falcon*, toward the desert planet of Tatooine. Han and his copilot, a Wookiee named Chewbacca, were returning there with some much-needed supplies for their friend Luke Skywalker.

Tatooine was suffering a severe drought. So Luke and a crew of scientists and engineers were building a super-vaporator there. It would supply Tatooine, Luke's home planet, with the water it needed to survive.

On board the *Falcon*, Chewbacca was playing Planetary Poker with a clever little robot named Artoo Detoo. Suddenly Artoo's computer monitor went dead. He stopped playing.

Chewbacca didn't like being ignored, especially when he was winning a game. He let out a stream of angry noises to attract Han Solo's attention.

"Forget that silly game, Chewie," said Han. "It's been a while since that robot was worked on. He could probably use some oil. But hurry. We're approaching Tatooine and I need your help to land this ship!"

Chewbacca looked around the ship, whining and growling all the while. Finally, he found a can of oil they had picked up the last time they were on Tatooine. He carefully shot a few drops of oil onto all of Artoo's joints. With a burst of blinking lights and a stream of bleeps and beeps, Artoo Detoo's monitor came back on. He rocked back and forth—seemingly out of control!

As Chewie jumped back to get out of his way, the berserk robot spun around and raced to the master computer controls of the *Millennium Falcon.*

Before Chewie or Han could stop the little robot, he plugged into the controls and turned the starship upside-down. Then the ship began turning wild somersaults!

Stunned, Solo and Chewie held on to their seats. Han was an experienced pilot, but try as he might, he could not gain control of his ship. So he put in an urgent call for help to Luke Skywalker on Tatooine.

Luke Skywalker watched his monitor closely as he tried to take ground-to-space control of the troubled ship.

"I cannot understand it, sir," said See Threepio, the mild-mannered robot who had been Artoo's interpreter and companion for many years. "Artoo has never acted like this before!"

"I don't understand it either, Threepio," said Luke. "I checked Artoo myself before the *Falcon* left. But I can't do anything from down here. I'll have to go up there and help them down."

Luke ordered his own plane to be brought to the hangar and quickly got ready to make an emergency rescue in space.

Luke was the son of a Jedi knight, one of the good and just warriors of the old days. Like the Jedi knights, Luke had been trained to use a special power called the Force. Though he did not yet know how to use its full power, he trusted his instincts and let the Force take over.

With the help of
the mysterious Force,
Luke Skywalker reached
the *Millennium Falcon*
and guided it back
to Tatooine.

Back on the ground, Han Solo shook Luke's hand while Chewie stood by, grinning. "We couldn't have done it without you, kid," said Han. "For a minute there, I thought we were all goners!"

"I was glad I could help you," said Luke with a smile. "Besides, we need those supplies for the super-vaporator. We've been having all kinds of problems here!"

Luke asked Threepio to take Artoo Detoo to Maintenance to be checked out. "We're having a conference in just a few minutes, Han," said Luke. "I'd like you and Chewie to come along and give a report on the trouble you had with Artoo."

Meanwhile, all the best scientists and technicians on Tatooine were talking in the conference room. Though they had checked all possible systems, not one of them could discover the cause of all the mechanical problems.

In the past week, computers had been breaking down. Robots had gone haywire and rebelled. Machine parts had been stolen or fooled with. Worst of all, the crew working on the vaporator project had found that several of the most important pieces had simply disappeared.

Someone was obviously trying to wreck the project! But no one had been able to find out who!

Everyone listened as Han Solo described
what had happened to Artoo Detoo aboard the
Millennium Falcon. Finally Captain Egoreg, leader
of the vaporator project, shook his head sadly.
"We cannot find a cause for all these mechanical
failures," he said. "I'm afraid that we will have to
give up our plans to bring water, and new life,
to Tatooine."

"But we can't just give up!" cried Princess Leia,
a young member of the intergalactic government.
"The people of Tatooine need our help to . . ."

Suddenly, in a flash of light and smoke,
the conference room exploded.

Luckily no one was seriously injured, though they were all quite shaken up. Captain Egoreg immediately ordered everyone to stop work on the vaporator project.

"I'll be the first one out of here!" cried Han Solo. "This place has gone crazy!"

Threepio seemed to be worse off than the others. He was rushed down to Maintenance for repairs.

Artoo Detoo was still there, shut down and waiting to be serviced. Threepio had decided to take a refreshing oil bath. He came out of the bath feeling even worse than he had right after the explosion. When he tried to speak to Artoo, no words came out!

Another R2 unit, a maintenance robot, quickly plugged his own computer into one of Threepio's checkpoint terminals. His lights started blinking on and off and he bleeped and beeped excitedly. He had discovered Threepio's problem. The oil supply was badly contaminated! Then he checked Artoo and found that his problem was oil contamination, too. The maintenance robot quickly cleared the systems of Artoo and Threepio.

The three robots hurried to tell Captain Egoreg what they had found out. But as they passed through the next room, they surprised a small group of jawas, the subhuman inhabitants of Tatooine. They were gibbering as they worked, and their red eyes glowed under their cloaks.

The robots rushed forward, startling the jawas, who ran in every direction. In the scuffle, Threepio and the maintenance robot were knocked to the floor. Luckily, Artoo managed to hook up with an alarm and send out a call for help!

Chewbacca, Luke, and Han Solo were the first to answer the call. They ran to Maintenance . . . and bumped into the wildly fleeing jawas. *"Catch them, Chewie!"* shouted Han.

With an ear-splitting roar, Chewie leaped through the air . . . catching all of the frightened creatures in one swoop!

Everyone knew that the jawas made their living selling old machines and used robots as junk. But they had become greedy for bigger profits. They started stealing mechanical parts and selling them to the innocent farmers on Tatooine.

Finally the jawas found that good machines could be turned into junk more quickly if they fooled with the parts and contaminated the oil the machines ran on. And that is just what they had been up to! Now they would be punished, and the work on the super-vaporator would continue as planned.

Chewie gave a growl of pleasure when Princess Leia
presented him with a reward for his bravery. Han Solo
patted him proudly on the back. As for Luke,
See Threepio, and Artoo Detoo—they were just happy
that the mystery was solved and all the trouble was over!